C 2

Take a

Story by Audrey Danforth and Jane Kennedy
Illustrations by Kristine Dillard

Jody loves to sing.
She loves to sing in the kitchen.
Her mother loves to listen.

She loves to sing on the bus.
Her friends love to listen.

3

She loves to sing in school.
Her teacher loves to listen.

She loves to sing on the phone.

Her grandparents love to listen.

She loves to sing in the shower.
Her dog loves to listen.

She loves to sing in the yard.
Everyone loves to listen.
Take a bow, Jody.